D1238892

Symbols of Our Country

I See the Bald Eagle

Harper Avett

illustrated by
Aurora Aguilera

PowerKiDS press

New York

Published in 2017 by The Rosen Publishing Group, Inc.
29 East 21st Street, New York, NY 10010

First Edition

Managing Editor: Nathalie Beullens-Maoui
Editor: Caitie McAneney
Book Design: Michael Flynn
Illustrator: Aurora Aguilera

Library of Congress Cataloging-in-Publication Data

Names: Avett, Harper, author.
Title: I see the bald eagle / Harper Avett.
Description: New York : PowerKids Press, [2017] | Series: Symbols of our
  country | Includes index.
Identifiers: LCCN 2016025482| ISBN 9781499427639 (pbk.) | ISBN 9781499430516
  (library bound) | ISBN 9781499429527 (6 pack)
Subjects: LCSH: Bald eagle–Juvenile literature. | Emblems,
  National–Juvenile literature. | Signs and symbols–Juvenile literature. |
  United States–Seal–Juvenile literature.
Classification: LCC QL696.F32 A94 2017 | DDC 598.9/43–dc23
LC record available at https://lccn.loc.gov/2016025482

Manufactured in the United States of America

CPSIA Compliance Information: Batch #BW17PK: For Further Information contact Rosen Publishing, New York, New York at 1-800-237-9932

Contents

Today my class is going on a field trip.

We're going to the zoo!

First, we see elephants and lions.

Then, I spot a bald eagle.

The bald eagle has a white head and brown body. It has long wings.

9

The bald eagle also has a yellow beak.
It has yellow eyes, too.

I ask my teacher about the bald eagle. She says it's a very special bird!

13

The bald eagle is the national bird of the United States.

My teacher says bald
eagles are strong birds.

They're very big, too.

Eagles stand for freedom.

They can fly high in the sky!

My teacher shows
me a quarter.

There's an eagle on the back.

The bald eagle is a symbol of America.

I'm lucky to have seen one!

Words to Know

beak

quarter

wing

Index